SUNDAY FUNDAY

Nicholas Bozza

Fulton Books, Inc.
Meadville, PA

Published by Fulton Books 2021

ISBN 978-1-63710-638-9 (paperback)
ISBN 978-1-63710-639-6 (digital)

Printed in the United States of America

This book is dedicated to the people who have inspired my journey through life:
For Eileen, who is not only my wife, but the constant source of motivation for me to follow my dreams.
For my aunts and uncles who have fostered a love of family tradition and pride in my Italian heritage.
and for Grandmom Mazzuca, who is probably still making meatballs in Heaven for Sunday Funday.

When I was growing up, Sundays were always a special time because it was when my aunts, uncles, and cousins filled my little house in the tree-lined neighborhood where I lived. Because we always had so much fun, my mama always called it "Sunday Funday!"

Every Sunday morning, my family woke up to the smell of coffee brewing in a pot and Frank Sinatra playing on the radio. After brushing my teeth and getting dressed, I sat at the kitchen table where Mama made breakfast for us. The kitchen was filled with all kinds of food on Sunday mornings because, after church, it was then that my mama would make her tomato gravy and meatballs for our Sunday Funday dinner.

Soon, it was time for church. Grandma put on her hat, and Mama put on her kerchief, and all of us piled into Daddy's blue car to drive to mass. Church was nice, but you had to sit still for a long time, and sometimes that's really hard for a kid to do. Sometimes I went with Grandma to light her candles, and she would hold my hand and whisper a quiet prayer in my year. I loved Grandma's prayers.

After church, sometimes Daddy would stop at Spatola's Bakery across the street from the church to buy some pastries to eat. Oh, how we loved going there! The bakery smelled yummy, and it always made me hungry.

"I'll have some cannoli, please," Daddy would say. "They are for our Sunday Funday." When our family came home, my mama put on her apron and took out the big pot to make her gravy while Grandma helped out by mixing the meat and added the ingredients for the meatballs.

"Angel," Mama would ask, "can you go outside and get some basil leaves from the garden? I need a nice handful."

Well, I loved being helpful, so I went out to the backyard garden that my daddy planted and counted out seven huge basil leaves. Once I came back inside, the basil leaves were added to the big pot of Mama's gravy.

While the gravy was simmering on the stove, my mama reached into the cabinet and took out a cast-iron skillet, filled it with oil, and fried the meatballs. They were so yummy, and the house smelled so good! Sometimes I asked Mama if I could try a meatball, but she would say that they were for Sunday Funday. Then Grandma would smile and would give me one to sample.

"You like-a the meat-a-balls, eh? Here, I give-a you one, but don't you tell-a you mama, okay?" she would say in her Italian accent. My smile would be the answer she was looking for!

Soon, many family members would arrive for Sunday Funday. Lots of aunts, uncles, and cousins piled into our little home. There was Uncle Dominick who smoked a cigar and wore a fedora cap, and Aunt Katie who always wore a pretty necklace. When Uncle Dominick came over to visit everyone, he gave the kids fifty cents each if we were good boys or girls. Then came Aunt Annie and

Uncle Zukes, along with their kids. Then, usually, the last ones to come over were Uncle Joe and Aunt Lena. Uncle Joe was a big man with a bald head and scruffy beard. He was such a funny man and always liked to play jokes on the kids. One thing that we all knew was that being together was a great way to celebrate Sunday Funday!

At 2:00 p.m., everyone sat down for a huge dinner of spaghetti, meatballs, sausage, and bread. After dinner, the kids would play games like hide-and-seek and ride our bikes around the neighborhood. Sometimes we would wait for the ice-cream man to come around so that we could buy vanilla cones with sprinkles. It was always so much fun on Sunday afternoons, and everyone would agree that it really was Sunday Funday after all.

When the kids went out to play, the ladies would sit in the kitchen and drink tea, tell stories, and share recipes. While they were in the kitchen, the men went into the backyard and drank glasses of wine as they looked at the backyard garden.

"You have so many figs on your tree," Uncle Dominick would say, "but your tomato plants are not growing much."

Uncle Dominick would talk about how to have a better vegetable garden, just like he had back in Italy. Soon, everyone else would give their ideas too!

At dusk, everyone went home, and it was time for me to take a bath and put my pajamas on. Once we were all settled for the night, everyone went into the parlor and had a snack of fruit and Jell-O. Then Daddy and I would watch *The Wonderful World of Disney* on TV and snuggle on the couch. Sometimes Mama would sit on the other couch and crochet. It was moments like these that made everyone feel peaceful on Sunday Funday.

Before you knew it, it was bedtime, but before I went to my room, I made sure my bag was packed for school in the morning, brushed my teeth, and said my prayers. I kissed Mama, Daddy, and Grandma good night and went to bed happy, already thinking about the next Sunday Funday!

CPSIA information can be obtained
at www.ICGtesting.com
Printed in the USA
BVHW022115060721
611232BV00014B/1552